IF IT CAN'T BE YOU

LOVE IN LOUISVILLE
BOOK 1.5

LILIANA WOODLAND

LILY WOODLAND PRESS

Cover Design: Audrey Halliwell

Paperback ISBN: 979-8-9959523-2-9

 Formatted with Vellum

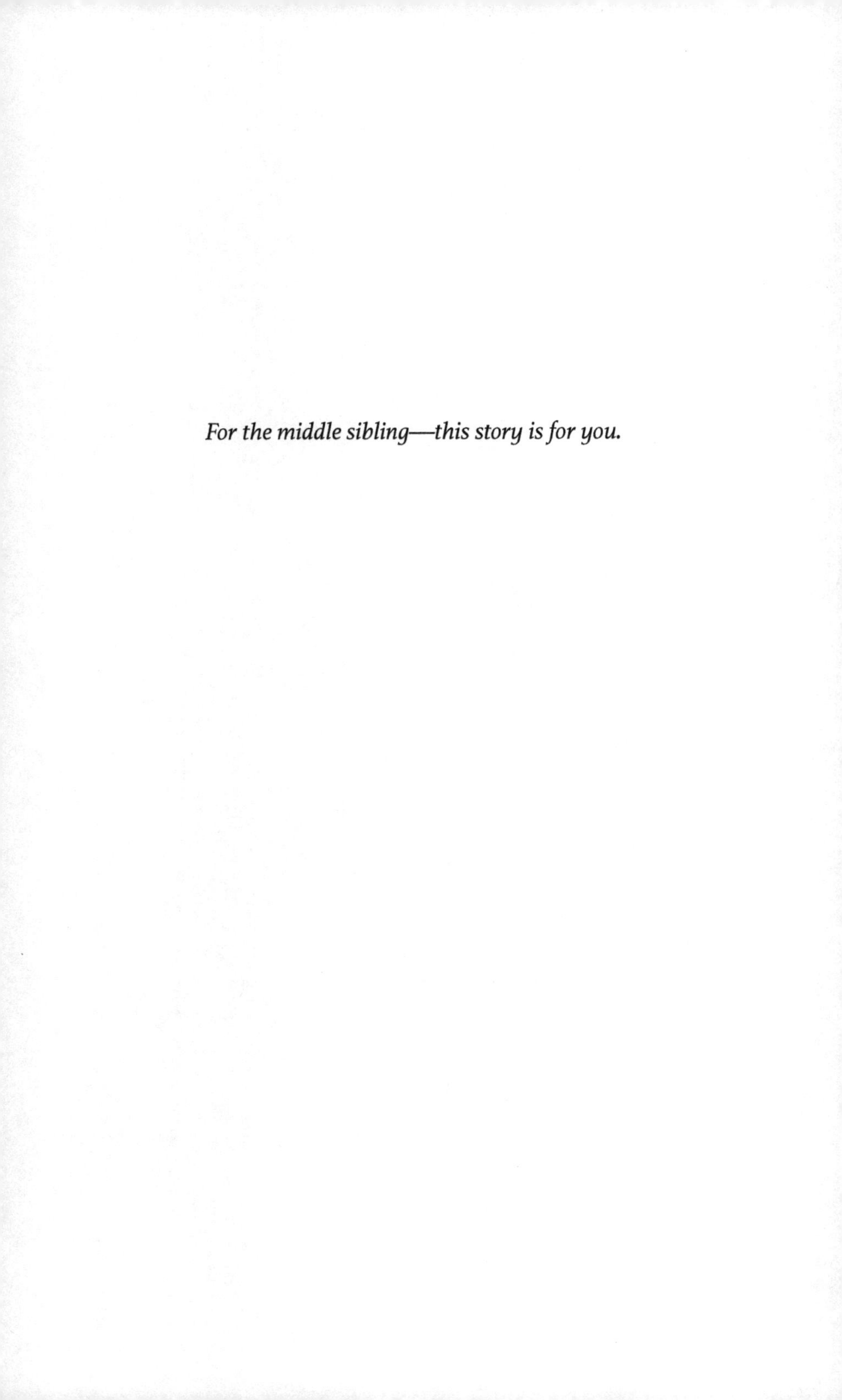

For the middle sibling—this story is for you.

AUTHOR'S NOTE

I want to start by thanking my beta readers and sensitivity readers, who were invaluable in helping me bring this story to life.

This story features two characters from my first book, *Exactly As You Are,* but it can definitely be read as a standalone. If you want a richer backstory for these two, however, you can pick up that book.

As for content warnings, there aren't a lot, but this story does contain explicit sexual content and swearing/language.

Thanks for being here, and happy reading!

1

————

CHRISTINE

I just fucked up big time.

I, Christine Lucille Coleman, asked the internet stranger I've been chatting with for months if he wants to meet up.

My breath stalls. The whoosh of the heat kicking on punctuates the silence. The rich scent of hazelnut coffee—decaf, because it's eight in the evening and I don't need to be awake all night—reaches my nose when I finally inhale. I'm alone in my bedroom, sitting on my bed, avoiding the basket of laundry at my back, as I wait for his response with the lightheadedness of a swooning Victorian lady. My heart trips over itself.

I don't really know the guy. Well, I feel like I do, but I've never seen him. He's in Louisville, Kentucky, like me, and he has a younger brother who lives out of state. I know he wasn't born in the US. He's thirty years old to my twenty-six. I've collected some other personal details about him, filing them away like little pieces of treasure.

I also know I've developed intense feelings for him. We've been talking for several months, a series of near-nightly conversations that feel like the most honest thing in my life, and I've done what I wasn't supposed to do when I downloaded this friendship app: decide I'm interested in romance instead.

> **ST_Louisville**
> I'm not sure.

> **ST_Louisville**
> I've loved our talks so, so much, I really have.
> I would be open to meeting you as a friend at
> some point, but I have to say, I'm interested
> in someone else. I need to be upfront about
> that. Maybe I'm being presumptuous, and
> you didn't mean to suggest a date.

Fuck. Rejection washes over me, sharp and intrusive. I had hoped he would be feeling the same fluttery want as me, but apparently not. Which is fine. Or it will be.

> **YourFriendLucy:**
> I understand. I'm happy to keep talking to
> you. I just wanted to throw the idea out there.

> **YourFriendLucy:**
> That I would be willing to meet, I mean. As a
> friend.

I lower my head into my hands, then drop my phone like it might burn me. At least I know now. The man I've been fantasizing about, picturing as someone I might fall in love with, wants someone else. It's ridiculous to be this upset when I haven't even seen him. For all I know, he might meet me wearing of those FBI: Female Body Inspector T-shirts and then I would never recover.

I like him so much, though. It's bordering on an unhealthy fixation.

Our connection has been nothing short of life-changing for me. I have a huge family, including three siblings and parents who live near me, a roommate I get along with, amicable relationships with my coworkers, and a few other friends, but sometimes I'm so damn lonely I can't stand it. And look, I know other people would kill to have what I have—a steady job, people who love me—but something is missing. I come across as pleasant or perhaps lovingly snarky with those I'm close with, but I feel like there's nothing to me, like one good swipe with a washcloth is all it would take to erase my entire personality. No one really *knows* me, myself included.

Hence, downloading the friendship app, Bee Friendly, though I didn't put my picture or too much personal info on my profile. Mostly I hoped to talk to some new people, to figure out who I am with someone who doesn't already have an impression of me. Instead, I'm harassing a man who thought I was his friend.

I pick my phone up again.

ST_Louisville
Are you okay with tabling that idea for now?

YourFriendLucy
Of course

ST_Louisville
I would love to keep talking to you, though.
This has been fun.

ST_Louisville
You should go back to your questions. The
get-to-know-you list you found

He's giving me an out, and I'm glad to have it. We can go back to our normal. I find my list, the one I have saved in the notes on my phone and pull up the next question.

> **YourFriendLucy**
> Okay. This one's a little dark. Can you remember a moment in your life when you were terrified?

> **ST_Louisville**
> Hmmm. I have a few, I guess. My memories of moving to the states at six years old are all a little scary. I was really young but I still remember those flashes of utter panic over being in a brand-new country. Of learning the language. It's not a single moment, but still.

> **ST_Louisville**
> What about you?

> **YourFriendLucy**
> Wow. Yours does sound really scary. I hope your classmates were nice to you

> **ST_Louisville**
> It's okay. I had a rough year, but there were lots of good moments too.

> **YourFriendLucy**
> I hope so. For me, it's probably this accident a couple of my family members were in earlier this year. That phone call...I still remember how it felt to hear my mom crying so hard I could barely understand her.

> **YourFriendLucy**
> The worst part was feeling so useless.

ST_Louisville
That's terrible, Lucy. I'm really sorry. No one
knows what to do in those situations, though.
You leave it up to the medical professionals.
I'm sure you being there was the most
important thing.

My sister, Joan, had known what to do. Everyone in my family has a role, and sometimes mine is just "whiny little sister." I don't say that to him.

ST_Louisville
Is everyone okay now, I hope?

YourFriendLucy
They're doing well, yeah. Thanks for asking.

YourFriendLucy
Next question.

ST_Louisville
I'm ready

YourFriendLucy
Tell me something you're really awful at.

ST_Louisville
Easy. Singing. It's cover your ears bad.

YourFriendLucy
You stole mine! How dare you. Not a musical
bone in my body.

ST_Louisville
If we do meet, maybe we'll go for karaoke.
Should be interesting

ST_Louisville
Or who knows? Maybe we've met before

> **YourFriendLucy**
> In a city of over six hundred thousand
> people? I doubt it.

> **ST_Louisville**
> Wow. Did you have to look that up?

> **YourFriendLucy**
> No. I like numbers, and I have this weird quirk
> about remembering city populations. And no,
> I will not expand on that.

> **ST_Louisville**
> Ha. Hey, no judgment. We've all got our thing.

> **ST_Louisville**
> I've got to go, though. Good night, math girl.
> Until we meet again.

> **YourFriendLucy**
> Good night, friend.

I fall to my back with an exasperated sigh. A stray clothes hanger jabs at my shoulder blade, but I don't move.

Sometimes he's flirty, and it confuses me. Though I could be misinterpreting him. I'm aware, in some part of my mind, that he could be lying about who he is. It's possible he's not in Louisville, or that he's not the age he claims to be. Our conversations feel authentic, though, and even if we are both holding back, I think he's being truthful about the things he's told me so far. At this point, I don't really care what he looks like. He's smart, funny, and kind, and that's all I need to know.

Maybe I could experiment with revealing more personal information. I've used an avatar instead of a real profile pic because I was nervous about the whole thing, but eventually, the goal should be making real-life friends, right? That's why I downloaded the app.

I push my fists into my eyes. What a mess I've created for myself.

The restaurant I'm in boasts the kind of sexy look that makes me want to pretend I'm someone else: sleek, modern lines, warm woods, dark windows, low lights courtesy of wooden, bell-shaped chandeliers. The Korean steakhouse is a special occasion sort of place.

My sister sits across from me, making eyes at her new boyfriend, Lucas, who happens to be her best friend of ten years. It shocked everyone, me more than any, but honestly, it works.

She looks at me. "Thanks for the new earrings, sis." She cups one with her hand.

"My pleasure," I say, meaning it. "You're only twenty-nine once."

My sister is, hands down, one of my favorite people on the planet. She admitted recently to feeling like our family asks too much of her, and I felt absolutely awful about it. I've watched her give so much of herself to our siblings, our parents, the rest of her extended family over the years, and I never stopped to ask if she felt too much pressure. I've been trying to be a better younger sibling, even if it's just giving her permission to step back. She doesn't need to tie herself in knots trying to take care of everyone.

She wanted something small for her birthday, so there are only four of us here tonight. She's usually surrounded by people. The intimacy of this is nice, especially given how large our family and friend group is, and I want to bask in the quality time with her.

Eric clears his throat next to me and drums his fingers on the table. "You look nice," he says to me.

Lucas's friend Eric—Mr. Takahashi to his students—spends a lot of time with Joan and Lucas, so I wasn't surprised when Joan mentioned he'd be here.

Joan and Lucas are in their own world again, so I turn to Eric. His brown eyes track over my face. I'm in a sweater dress and knee-high boots, my hair arranged and swept to one side with the help of my roommate, Angela. I catch Eric's gaze dipping down to my thighs for a quick second.

Eric is into me. I'm not conceited—he's just that expressive, and I can pick up on the signs even if he's trying to conceal it. If Joan hadn't told me, I would have figured it out. I don't know what to do with it. He's not making me feel pressure, like I owe him anything, but this simmering tension exists anyway. Given how often we both hang out with my sister and her boyfriend, I see him frequently.

And look, he's hot. Really hot. His angular jaw lends him a rugged masculine appeal, though his wide smile is almost boyish. The combination is powerful. He has the whitest teeth I've ever seen—toothpaste commercial-worthy—an olivey tan complexion, and spiky black hair I can imagine running my fingers through. I'm a tall gal, and he's a little taller than me, which isn't a requirement but is a nice bonus. And he looks at me like he could *devour* me. I don't think I've ever been the recipient of such open, unabashed interest before.

Unfortunately, I can't get my mystery man out of my mind. It's stupid, but I don't feel very available right now, even though I am.

"Thanks." My eyes flick over him. His leg muscles do look nice in his slacks. When I return his stare, he's wearing a knowing smile. My face heats. "So do you." I gesture to Joan and Lucas. "You think they know we're here?"

Lucas—goofy, animated, gregarious Lucas—is telling Joan a story with liberal use of his hands. She laughs at him, her head tipped back like he's the funniest person she's ever met.

"We might as well be light fixtures," Eric says. His body angles toward mine, his thighs spreading so that one leg brushes mine. A little warmth pools in my abdomen. "So how was your week? Work's been good?"

"Ha. An accountant talking about their work is like watching paint dry, don't you think?"

"I really want to know," he says. His smile blinds me for a moment.

"It was good." I take a sip of my wine. "I got to look at spreadsheets. You would perish from excitement if I went into more detail."

"You love data, though, right? You told me that once."

"I can't believe I admitted that. But yes, I get inappropriately enthusiastic about data."

"I think it's brave that you talk about your geeky obsessions." He rubs a hand along his smooth jaw to hide his smile.

I lay my hand on my chest in mock offense. "I would think someone who talks about covalent bonds all day might be a little more understanding." I lean a little closer to him. "Speaking of which, how's the teacher life?"

"It's good. I think a few of my students actually listen to me, so that helps."

"Oof. That sounds like a low bar. Do you ever wish you'd done something else, then?"

"Nah. I love teaching. There's something so rewarding about knowing you're responsible for a young person's understanding of a complex topic. Though, I will say that you've never experienced a real burn until a high schooler insults you."

I laugh. "Yeah? Let's hear it."

"It was the class clown. He told me I have a personality like a sentient piece of toast."

"For what it's worth, I would be friends with a nice piece of toast."

He chuckles, his eyes never leaving mine. This is the third time I've seen him in two weeks, though we're always with other people, and the way he holds my gaze remains the same on each occasion: with a singular focus, like the room could be on fire and he would still want to look at me.

"It was funny how I wanted to defend myself," he says. "I found myself thinking I should show this high-schooler how much fun I have when I'm not teaching. Like, I have pictures, even."

"I'll vouch for you," I say. "If you need me to show up one day and talk about our bowling league."

"There's no way my students would believe we're friends. You're way too cool."

"Last night I watched a two-hour documentary about the life of an octopus on my living room couch."

"Yes, but somehow that makes you even cooler," he says. "I can't explain it."

I laugh. "I'm an accountant in my twenties who hasn't been on a date in six months. Trust me, you are the *only* person who thinks I'm cool."

I regret it as soon as the words leave my mouth. His face slackens as though he's surprised, then he opens his mouth like he's gearing up to say something.

Lucas taps his spoon against his glass. "To Joan," he says, raising his glass, and I join in, glad for the distraction. Joan winks at me when I toast her.

"Happy birthday to the best sister," I say.

"You're so full of shit." Joan laughs and sips her own wine.

We stay late, eating dessert and chatting until well into the night. Eric walks me to my car after I've said my goodbyes to Joan and Lucas.

It's cold out, and he moves closer to me when we approach my vehicle. He props one hand against my car.

"Can I ask you something?" His eyes search my expression.

My limbs tense. I know what's coming, and I don't know how to respond yet, but I nod anyway.

"You know I like you."

God. He's fucking brave. I'm momentarily turned on by his candor despite myself.

"I mean, yeah." I bite my lip, and he watches. "I'm aware." I cock my head. "I haven't been trying to play with your feelings or anything, I swear. I do enjoy your company."

He groans and rubs a hand over his face. "'I enjoy your company' is maybe the blandest thing you could say about someone. I guess piece-of-toast guy had a point." He holds up a hand to forestall my objections. "I knew you didn't feel exactly the same way. It's why I've hesitated the past few months. But I thought back there," he tilts his head toward the restaurant, "we maybe had a little something going. And I was hoping we could get dinner together again. Alone, I mean."

Damn. I *hate* being in this position. He's sweet, attractive, and smart. He's close friends with my sister's boyfriend, so double dates would be easy. I'm holding back, though, and I know why. The stranger I've been talking to has a grip on my feelings, even though he's already rejected a meet-up.

Eric reads my hesitation and backs up a little. My heart squeezes.

"It's okay, Christine. It's just that I never actually made my feelings explicit, and nothing will happen if I'm too afraid to make a move. Just so you know, the invitation's there."

He starts to turn, and I reach for the sleeve of his wool coat. "Wait," I say.

He's still as a picture. A gust of wind blows his inky hair over his forehead.

I cross my arms over my chest. "There's someone else I'm interested in. I have pretty strong feelings for him."

He flinches, and a prick of guilt needles my insides. He's so easy to read, even if he wouldn't give voice to his hurt. I owe him honesty, though.

"I don't think it's going to work out. Me and this other

person," I say. "So I'll go to dinner if you're okay with knowing I'm not quite there yet. I totally understand if you aren't cool with that."

He gives a tight shrug. "I'll have to think about it."

Ouch. This conversation is hurting both of us. Was it inevitable? Did I do something wrong here? I'm all mixed up now.

"Yeah," I say. "I figured. I'm so sorry, Eric."

He waves that off. "I'm glad to know, at least." He walks backward, still looking at me. "Night, Christine."

"Goodnight, Eric."

2

ERIC

My head thunks against the headrest in my car when I get in. I really fucked that up, but what can I say? The ambiance in the restaurant must have gotten to me. The dim lighting, the fancy tablecloth, the way Christine's golden brown hair fell in soft waves over her shoulder—it felt like romance, and my brain short-circuited.

I need to move past this burning, unrequited thing I have for Christine. It wouldn't be that hard to distance myself from her—I hang out with Lucas a lot, but I can see him without Christine around. If I take her up on her friendly dinner offer, it will just make things worse.

I drive back to my apartment, still chastising myself as I go. I made her uncomfortable, and I hate that. Then again, I can't keep seeing her, trying and failing to adopt outward stoicism while I burn with fiery longing. It's not fair to either of us.

Once I've shucked my coat and tossed it on the couch, I unbutton a few of the top buttons on my shirt and lean back in my recliner.

The offer from the mystery lady, the stranger on the friendship app, comes back to me. I can tell she's interested in more with me, even though I played it off. We've been chatting for months, falling deeper into our digital connection, and I know at some point we should move toward a real-life meeting, but I'm holding back for several reasons. The first one is Christine, which is, as I've seen, misguided. But also, chatting with the woman on the app has been easy, a nice way to unwind, and I don't want to complicate it.

I push the button for the app.

> **ST_Louisville**
> You around? How's your night going?

It takes a few minutes, but she responds.

> **YourFriendLucy:**
> Absolute shit. You?

> **ST_Louisville**
> Same.

I sigh. Talking to her does soothe some of the jagged edges of my disappointment. I know I should be careful given how I suspect she feels about me, but I really have loved our conversations.

I joined a few months ago when I was feeling restless. At the time, I was contemplating moving away from Louisville. Nothing is pinning me here other than my ill-advised crush on Christine. My parents and brother are in Virginia, which isn't that far away, but it takes several hours to make the drive. I have some other relatives scattered across the US, and some back in Japan, but in this city I just have the circle of friends and acquaintances I've found for myself. There's nothing wrong with it, but sometimes I crave a deeper connection. Hence the app, and my friendship with the mystery lady.

YourFriendLucy
So what happened to your night?

ST_Louisville
Just love life woes. Or lack of a love life, I
suppose

YourFriendLucy
Ah. The woman you're interested in?

ST_Louisville
Yeah. I don't think it's going to work out.

I stop there, unsure how much more I want to share. Revealing more personal information feels like it would break the spell.

ST_Louisville
And you?

YourFriendLucy
Also love life woes

That's intriguing. Maybe I misread her interest in me. Which would be a good thing, really.

ST_Louisville
Sorry. I'll pour one out for our mutual failures.

YourFriendLucy
It's okay. I'm just in a weird situation

YourFriendLucy
I do have some good news, though—I got a
bonus at work! So I've been pumped about
that. I should probably do something smart
with it, but I'm thinking of treating myself to
some new clothes.

ST_Louisville
You know, I think the idea you have to be smart with money all the time is utter bullshit. I budget, but I also spend money on stupid things. It's worth the occasional dopamine hit.

ST_Louisville
So what is it you do? Are we allowed to share that?

YourFriendLucy
I guess we haven't talked about it, have we? What's your guess?

ST_Louisville
Paranormal investigator?

YourFriendLucy
Close. I'll give you a little hint—it involves working with money

ST_Louisville
Banking? Corporate finance?

ST_Louisville
Professional gambling?

YourFriendLucy
I think I'll let you stew on that for a while. What about yours?

ST_Louisville
My hint is that it involves science.

YourFriendLucy
That's fun. I've got some thoughts.

ST_Louisville
Yeah?

YourFriendLucy
Marine biology?

ST_Louisville
Ah, yes. Seeing as Kentucky is famously near
an ocean

YourFriendLucy
I'm looking that up. I bet there are some who
live around here.

YourFriendLucy
Deodorant tester?

ST_Louisville
You sure know a lot about science

I heave myself out of the recliner, smiling now, to get a glass of water. I don't know what it is that draws me to this stranger. She's kind, yes, and funny, but it's also easy to be vulnerable with her. Not with specifics about our lives—we don't really go into those—but in how we feel about different things. I don't have a lot of people in my life who fill that role. Despite all my friendships, I often feel I have surface-level relationships with everyone, and it's hard for me to open up, even as someone who likes people.

I turn the television on, then shuffle to my room to change clothes before settling back into my recliner again.

ST_Louisville
Okay, so specific jobs are off the table, I
guess. New topic. We talked about the things
we suck at. What are you good at?

YourFriendLucy
Hmm. Why is this so much harder?

ST_Louisville
That inner critic is loud.

YourFriendLucy
For sure. Okay, I'll try. Sports and math. Those
are my things. Basketball especially. I played
in high school

> **ST_Louisville**
> Interesting. I've been picturing you as short.
> Not that you couldn't play basketball as a
> short woman, but still.

YourFriendLucy
I'm 5'10". Sorry to disappoint you there

> **ST_Louisville**
> There's nothing wrong with tall women. I
> happen to like them.

I think of Christine, who is nearly as tall as me, and her
long limbs. Clearly I'm into that. In my fantasies, her long legs
are wrapped around me, and her cheeks are flushed. I shake off
that image.

YourFriendLucy
What about you?

> **ST_Louisville**
> How tall am I? About 5'11". I'm considered
> kinda tall where I'm from

YourFriendLucy
Ooh, another hint. But that's actually not
what I was talking about. What I meant was
what are your talents?

> **ST_Louisville**
> Oh. Also sports—baseball particularly, but I
> also played a few different ones in high
> school. Ages ago, at this point, but I still play
> in some different leagues. Science, like I
> mentioned, and one branch more than
> others. And writing. I really enjoy writing.

YourFriendLucy
That's interesting. I'm not that great at
writing, so I'm always impressed with people
who are.

ST_Louisville
There are ways to improve, though. That's
part of what's fun about it

YourFriendLucy
Okay. How do I get better?

ST_Louisville
I like prompts. I've found a few online, and
they help you with story ideas. And with
crafting sentences.

YourFriendLucy
Alright. Hit me, then.

I ponder that. I have a folder where I've saved some of my
favorites, but I remember a few of them.

ST_Louisville
Here you go. I'll start easy. Fill in the blanks:
I'd love to ___but my ____ just ____

YourFriendLucy
I'd love to go, but my cat just vomited
everywhere

YourFriendLucy
What do you think?

ST_Louisville
Not bad.

ST_Louisville
Now finish this sentence. I believe in love,
but____

YourFriendLucy
I find myself standing over my husband's
dead body, knife in hand.

I bark out a laugh.

ST_Louisville
Jesus Christ.

YourFriendLucy
How did I do? I think I read too many thrillers.

YourFriendLucy
Now I can see why you don't want to meet up

ST_Louisville
Actually, that was very creative. And it got a
big laugh from me, so well done

ST_Louisville
Also, I didn't say no to meeting. I'm giving it
consideration.

My heart pounds against my ribcage. It scares me, allowing
this little bubble of safety out into the real world. There's something special about knowing each other like this, without
worrying about the impression we're making. Besides that, I
know making that decision will be the day I've decided to give
up on Christine. This stranger and I could have something,
maybe, if I let myself, if I can get over this intense yearning for
someone who doesn't want me back.

YourFriendLucy
I know, I know. Fave genre?

ST_Louisville
Sci-fi, definitely. I'll read anything that's even
in the ballpark. And I would love to publish
something in that genre someday.

ST_Louisville
You have any more questions for me? From
the list you found? I like those.

YourFriendLucy
Sure. I'm rooting for your writing career, by
the way.

YourFriendLucy
Although, eek. I'm skipping the next one.

I'm smiling as I reply.

ST_Louisville
No, you've got to tell me now.

YourFriendLucy
It's NSFW.

ST_Louisville
I don't mind. You've already threatened
murder, anyway. I'm not sure how much
weirder this can get.

YourFriendLucy
I wasn't threatening, I was just describing a
murder.

YourFriendLucy
Since you demanded it. What's your fave sex
position?

Okay, wow. I'm tempted to say "all of them." I've pictured it
with Christine in a hundred different ways: in my apartment, in
this very chair. Kneeling in front of her, spreading her thighs
for my mouth after I've pulled her to the edge of my bed. Her
on her knees in front of me. When it comes to her, my imagin-
ings are a series of x-rated scenes cobbled together and played
on a loop.

Though, to be clear, I also want to hold her at night and listen to her talk about spreadsheets. I'm a well-rounded guy.

God, I have problems.

If I'm going to get over Christine, this flirtation might not be a bad tactic. I type out a message and hit send before I can think too much about it.

3

CHRISTINE

> **ST_Louisville**
> I'm going to cheat a little and say I like going
> down on women. That's my favorite. Like, by a
> wide margin.

Holy. Hell.

I feel flushed, savoring the warmth spreading from my abdomen and pelvis, as I stare at his reply. A hundred different responses flit around in my mind, but I can't grab hold of one. I'm too flustered.

> **ST_Louisville**
> Sorry. Too far?

> **YourFriendLucy**
> I mean, if anything the question was too far
> on my part.

> **YourFriendLucy**
> But no, that's...really hot, actually.

My breath evaporates in my lungs as I hit send. My hands tremble in my lap. Is this for real? Are we doing this now?

I wait—and wait some more—and my God, I could have learned a new language in the time it's taking him to get back to me—before he finally says something.

> **ST_Louisville**
> I should pose the same question to you.

I type something, then shut my eyes when I hit send.

> **YourFriendLucy**
> Easy. I kinda like being on top.

I brush my fingers over my mouth. I can't believe I'm having this conversation with him after months of chatting. And it should feel reckless, talking about sex with him, but it doesn't. It seems like a natural extension of our bordering-on-flirty banter. Or it does to me, anyway.

> **ST_Louisville**
> I'm taking a few deep breaths here.

> **ST_Louisville**
> That certainly escalated.

> **YourFriendLucy**
> Too much?

> **YourFriendLucy**
> Sorry. I know you're interested in someone else. I didn't mean to cross a line with my question.

> **ST_Louisville**
> It's okay. I'm the one who answered you.
> That's actually kind of complicated, anyway.

> **ST_Louisville**
> No, scratch that. It's not complicated at all.
> I've been interested in her for a long time,
> and I learned she doesn't feel the same way.

YourFriendLucy
Oof. I'm sorry. Truly.

ST_Louisville
I ruined the moment with my sad sack
story, huh?

YourFriendLucy
Nah. No worries.

I set my phone down on the coffee table in my living room. The flush I was experiencing now feels sour, like I bit into what I thought was an apple and got a lemon instead. The bitter tinge of jealousy settles in my stomach.

The door to my apartment bangs open. Angela, my roommate, rushes in. She's chatting on her phone, saying goodbye to whoever is on the other end. Her sleek brown ponytail swings behind her.

She's the most energetic person I've ever met. She's not even five feet tall, so a literal foot shorter than me, and she's a little ball of enthusiasm, always roping me into trendy exercise classes and social outings. I don't mind too much. Despite being an accountant who spends inordinate amounts of time chatting with an internet stranger, I *am* an extrovert. She outpaces me by several miles per hour even on my best days, though.

"What wrong?" She puts her purse on the counter. "You look so sad. Have you been watching Charlotte's Web again?"

I force a melancholy smile. "You know the guy I've been talking to? The one from the app?"

"Of course. You've disappeared into that damn phone like Alice down the rabbit hole."

"You going to reference children's movies all night?"

Angela pulls her lips to one side. "Actually, I think I might."

She walks over to the fridge to grab a bottle of water. I lean onto the kitchen counter, propping my chin in my hands.

"He's interested in someone else. He only wants friendship with me. And it's fine. I just need to stop. It's like an addiction. I like him so much."

She sits at one of the kitchen barstools. "Aw. I'm sorry, babe. I know that hurts. He should be so lucky as to meet you." She pouts. "We should go somewhere. There's this new speakeasy place on Bardstown Road."

"You just got home." I laugh. "You've barely set foot in the door."

"All the more reason to turn around!" She grins at me.

"Actually, I think I'm going to bed."

She puts a hand on her hip. "Why don't you go out with someone else? Maybe you just need some other options. You've been holed up in here, mooning over this dude for months, and it's not going anywhere."

She's a little blunt, but she's not wrong. I've got to do something proactive to stop this incessant, hollow yearning.

I open the app on my phone again. After wishing Angela a good night and telling my mystery man goodbye, I shuffle to my room. A few articles of clothing lay strewn about, my bed's unmade, and empty cups clutter my nightstand. A mostly-spent candle leaves the room smelling like vanilla and burnt wick. My room's almost as big a mess as my personal life.

A wild impulse almost has me picking up my phone to text Eric. If things aren't going to work with my mystery man, maybe I should give him a chance. He deserves better than my reckless whims, though, and I don't want to jerk him around.

I flop back on my bed. Whatever I do about this, it has to be soon. I can't stand this longing any more.

4

ERIC

Christine's arm brushes against mine, and she aims a small smile at me that fills my chest with heat.

So much for moving on. I tried flirting with the mystery woman, and instead of it being exciting, I felt like I was being disloyal. Which is ridiculous, really. Christine's not torn up over me.

We're having dinner at Lucas's with a group of Joan and Lucas's friends. Everyone is laughing and talking around me, but I'm focused on the tiny point of physical contact between myself and Christine.

The food, an assortment of dishes we've all contributed, is delicious. I've brought vegetable yakisoba, a Japanese fried noodle recipe I pretend was easy when in actuality I had to call my mom and have her walk me through it. The atmosphere is buzzing with camaraderie. I like our circle of friends. Despite all that, I find myself wishing Christine and I were by ourselves, even though she doesn't want me.

I *hate* feeling like I would take anything she gives me. It seems wrong, somehow. Pathetic. But that's where I'm at.

She's so beautiful. She's wearing a fitted black shirt she's tucked into her jeans. Her hair's pinned back in a bun that lays against her neck. Her cheeks glow with a rosy bloom.

"I'm starving," Christine says after turning my way. "I could eat a horse." She cocks her head at me. "Although that's a weird phrase when you think about it."

I smile at her, reveling in her nearness, which tightens my nerves and sets my blood on fire. "There's a Japanese word," I tell her. "Kuchisabishii. It literally translates to 'lonely mouth,' and it's like, that urge to eat when you aren't really that hungry, or when you're bored, for example. I always liked that one."

She repeats the word, being careful with the pronunciation. "I love it," she says. "It's the perfect way to describe that feeling. Though right now, I really am starved."

We eat and socialize for a bit, and eventually some of us congregate in the open kitchen together. People filter in and out, and I find myself alone with Christine when most of the group gathers in front of the living room television to watch a football game. She props her hip against the kitchen island and inches closer to me. There's an easy athleticism to the way she moves, like she's gliding toward me. It's one thing that drew me to her—I like her humor and her sharp mind, but I've also loved watching her in our shared softball and bowling leagues.

My heart rate kicks up when she looks at me.

"Who are you rooting for?" She nods toward the television.

"I don't really care about the outcome of this one," I tell her. "I've got a few players for my fantasy league, though. It would be great if they could do well."

"Lucas won't shut up about how well he's doing in your league. So if you could beat him I would appreciate it." She smiles and cocks her head. "Did you play? In high school?"

"Football? Hell no. I love athletics, but I'm more of a non-violent sport kind of guy myself. I have no desire to get my head bashed in."

She wrinkles her nose. "I do have lots of concerns about the brutality of it. And the brain trauma."

"Same. And it's not like I'm some huge guy, either."

"I don't know. You're surprisingly muscly for a high school teacher," she says, glancing at my biceps in my short-sleeved black tee.

I fight the urge to flex, or perhaps find something nearby I can lift for her.

"You been spending some extra time at the gym?"

"Why, Christine," I say, smiling at her, "sounds like you might be stereotyping a bit."

"I don't remember any of my teachers looking like you," she says, and now my heart moves up to my throat. Is this flirting, what we're doing? I can't even trust my own judgment.

Before I can respond, more people enter the kitchen for drinks, and we're pulled apart again. I try to keep my gaze off her while I'm in the middle of other conversations, but it takes some effort.

At the end of the night, I'm surprised to find Christine beside me while I make my way to my car.

"Eric." She touches my sleeve.

Our friends' laughter drifts over to us as everyone is leaving. We haven't transitioned to winter yet, and the rich, earthy scent of fallen leaves reaches me. Christine herself smells like strawberries. A full moon hangs in the sky, casting a bit of luminous glow on us. We're inching closer to each other, and I'm reminded of our last dinner together, where it feels like I'm getting confusing signals. How do I proceed here?

"What is it?" I lean against my car, casual-like. I'm not fooling anyone. She can probably see my heart pounding in my chest.

"If that dinner invitation is still open, I want to go. If you decided you're okay with it, that is. I know you weren't sure the last time we talked." She's hesitant, and I find myself wanting to reassure her despite my own reservations.

"Is this a pity thing?"

"No!" She rushes to say it. "No. I wouldn't do that to you. I want to go."

This should be what I want to hear, but it feels a little hollow, like I've nagged her into a date somehow. That's not what happened, but I can't shake the icky feeling.

"Okay," I say. "So the other guy didn't work out?"

She winces. "He's into someone else. And I just feel...miserable, honestly. I'm being so stupid."

Well, that sounds familiar.

"I know what it sounds like," she says. "I want to give this a chance, though."

And how can I say no to that? My earlier hesitation had to do with her feelings for someone else, but she's in front of me, her eyes hopeful, and I can't turn her down.

"How about Thursday night?" I search her face. "I've got a restaurant in mind. A new Italian place."

"Alright." She smiles, and something melts in my brain, some vital piece of resistance I should probably be clinging to. "It's a date."

YourFriendLucy
I need to ask you something.

The recliner rocks as I shift in it. I scrub a hand over my forehead. A ribbon of guilt squeezes like a fist around my heart, though I'm not sure why. I'm only friends with this woman. Still, it feels different now that I'm actually going on a date with Christine.

I've spoken to the mystery lady several times a week for the last few months. Frankly, it would be stranger if we didn't talk.

> **ST_Louisville**
> Sure.

YourFriendLucy
Okay...I'm nervous about this.

YourFriendLucy
But I've had feelings for you for a while now. I know that's nuts, considering we've never met, but I feel connected to you in a way I've never experienced with anyone else. I know you're into someone else, but if there's any way you have an inkling of the same feelings, I want to know. I have someone else I might be starting something with, and I need some input on where you and I stand first.

Fuuckkk. I knew it, and having confirmation is good, but what the hell do I do with the information? I mean, I could like this woman if I allowed myself, if I weren't so hung up on Christine. Lucy, whoever she is, can't just be a backup, though. She deserves more than that.

> **ST_Louisville**
> Wow. That's really brave, Lucy.

YourFriendLucy
Ugh. Out of all the responses, that one is almost the worst.

YourFriendLucy
I mean, it's okay. I understand and I appreciate your honesty

ST_Louisville
I'm really sorry. I made a little progress with the woman I'm interested in, and I have to give this a chance. I like you a lot, though. I'll still meet you for coffee or something, because I really could use another friend. I've been looking for more reasons to stay in Louisville.

YourFriendLucy
This keeps getting worse and worse 😭

YourFriendLucy
I did ask, though. So that's on me.

ST_Louisville
If we both find ourselves single in a few weeks, we can come back to this. Maybe you can give whoever it is you're seeing a chance. I have to see this through with the woman I'm going out with—and I'm so sorry if it feels like I'm putting you on the back burner. I don't want to hurt you.

ST_Louisville
Besides, what if you don't like the way I look?

YourFriendLucy
I've thought about that. I think our connection has made that not even matter. If I think you're hot, that's just a bonus.

ST_Louisville
What if my skin is green?

YourFriendLucy
Is it? I'm intrigued.

YourFriendLucy
Like an ogre?

ST_Louisville
I do think it would put a damper on any
attraction.

ST_Louisville
What if I'm a robot?

YourFriendLucy
Oh God. I actually had that thought. If you're
some kind of artificial intelligence I'll be so
rattled I'll never sleep again.

ST_Louisville
I'm real.

YourFriendLucy
Sounds like something a machine would say.

YourFriendLucy
You wouldn't care what I look like, either?

I carry my phone to my bedroom. I'm smiling again despite
my discomfort with her admission. She's sweet, this woman.

ST_Louisville
I won't say that physical attraction means
nothing to me. The emotional stuff is better,
though. And I know we've had this great thing
going on. It's just, there's someone else
eclipsing that. If you want to stop talking, I
totally understand.

My breath freezes. I don't want to stop talking to my friend,
but I was serious about not wanting to hurt her, either.

YourFriendLucy
No, it's okay. We can still talk.

YourFriendLucy
Can we pretend that conversation never
happened, though?

ST_Louisville
Absolutely.

ST_Louisville
On that note, what have you been up to
tonight? Anything fun?

YourFriendLucy
I saw some of my family, actually. My siblings.

ST_Louisville
You said you're close to them, right?

YourFriendLucy
I am, yeah. I get a little lost in the shuffle
sometimes—it can be like that in a big family.
I have complicated feelings about it. Ugly
feelings, sometimes.

ST_Louisville
I promise I won't judge you.

YourFriendLucy
I don't know, you might. I have a younger
brother with a disability and he requires a lot
of support, so sometimes the rest of us get a
little overshadowed by that. I always feel bad
saying it, because he didn't ask for any of it,
and we love him dearly. Sometimes I wonder
what my identity is without the context of my
sibling relationships, though. And my older
sister is this caregiver type, so she helps out a
lot, but it doesn't come as naturally to me. It's
a complex situation.

YourFriendLucy
I love them, though. We're a team.

Something nudges at the back of my mind. There's a flicker
of recognition, like I've heard someone having this conversation
recently. I think about it as I change into a pair of loose shorts.

ST_Louisville
I don't doubt that you love them. And I don't think any differently of you, I promise. I've got my own issues with my family. Like all of us.

YourFriendLucy
Yeah?

ST_Louisville
Of course. My mom had breast cancer a couple years ago and she didn't tell me or my brother for a while. I know she thought her reasons were good, but it hurt us.

YourFriendLucy
God. I'm so sorry. Is she okay now?

ST_Louisville
She's doing alright, yeah. In remission.

I can't believe I just shared that. I recline on my bed, twirling my phone in my hand. Even some of my other close friends don't know about my mom. When she didn't want it shared, I felt like I shouldn't, either. But it was so scary it feels good to get it off my chest.

YourFriendLucy
I'm so, so glad to hear that.

She means it, I can tell. She seems like the type who cares for others.

YourFriendLucy
Well, I think I'm headed for bed. Good night, science boy.

ST_Louisville
Night, math girl.

5

CHRISTINE

"This is delicious."

I'm on a date with Eric. We're talking, laughing, bantering with each other. The conversation flows freely, the food is top-tier, and his shirt molds to his biceps in the most distracting manner. He smiles easily, too, and it keeps catching me by surprise, the way he grins like there's nowhere he'd rather be.

The table where we're seated is tiny. Our knees graze under the tablecloth, and he keeps aiming apologetic glances at me. He's so sweet it hurts. He's been charming, and adorable, and my reluctance here is bananas.

"I've been hearing about this place," Eric says. "I'm glad you like it."

"It really is an experience. I'll have to mention it to Wyatt. He was just talking about taking Jenny on a date for their anniversary." Wyatt's my older brother. I think Eric met him once when we were all together, but Wyatt's busy with his twin boys a lot, so he's not around as much.

"Yeah? And how are they, your family? I only ever see Joan."

"About the same." I shrug. "Ben's doing well now that he has a day program to go to again. Mom and Dad are happy."

Ben is my younger brother. I know it's hard to keep all the names straight, but Eric has taken the time to learn.

"And what about you?" He twirls some pasta on his fork, and the rich scent of butter hits me. "Are you happy?"

"I'm the neglected middle child," I say. "No one cares how I feel." I lift my hand when I see him start to comment on this. "I'm kidding. Mostly."

"Well, you're *my* favorite Coleman," he says. He pushes more noodles around on his plate. "And if it makes you feel any better, I think Ian might be currying more favor with my parents now, since he lives closer to them. I feel a little left out sometimes." Ian's *his* younger brother, and I've met him a couple times when he's been visiting. The two of them seem close, like me and my siblings.

"Do you wish you lived there, too?"

"I like it here." He's staring at me as his lips tilt up on one side, and I feel like he's saying *yes, I like it right here with you.* There's a moment where we look at each other, an unspoken understanding passing between us. "I have considered moving, but I've built a life in Louisville. Friendships. Career." He swallows. "That sort of thing."

The way he looks at me makes it hard to think. My thoughts are pinballs pinging around in my head without taking hold.

"I'm stuffed," I say, laying my fork down.

"Me too," he says. He sits back. "Speaking of my parents, they made me clean my plate as a kid. I still have this nagging feeling I shouldn't leave food, but I've allowed myself to do that as an adult." He rubs his hands along his thighs. "What's strange is that the last time I saw my parents at home, my mom just threw away some pork we didn't eat. I was shocked and appalled. That would have been forbidden when I was growing up."

I laugh. "It's so wild when they abandon their principles like that. You should see my parents with their grandsons. It's a whole new level of 'who are these people?' My nephews get to do whatever they want around them." My gaze finds his again. "You visit your parents often?"

His head tips from side to side. "Pretty often. It takes several hours to drive there. To Virginia, I mean." He inhales. "They've found some community with other Japanese folks there. It's nice, feeling that sense of connection."

"I can imagine how meaningful that is for them." I roll my lips together. "And you? Do you have that here in Louisville?"

"A bit. Maybe not as much as I would like," he admits. "But my parents are different. They moved to Virginia as adults, and I was just a little kid."

He smiles again, and my brain stalls. A lightning-quick flash of something like desire lights me up. I'm not going to examine that just yet.

"My parents are also the only people who call me by my given name," he continues.

"Ah. Seiya?" I've heard Lucas say it before. My brows pull in. "Which do you prefer?"

"Definitely Eric. That's what I've been as long as I can remember, and I like it." He laughs. "I had a coworker once who insisted on calling me Seiya all the time, like she was doing me some favor."

"Ew." I nudge my plate away from me. Another bite of pasta might literally kill me. "I'll never understand why people can't just call you what you ask them to call you." The lights seem to dim as we study each other. "I do like knowing it, though. Seiya. It's a great name."

His Adam's apple bobs with his swallow. "I like it when you say it, too. Feels...intimate."

My cheeks burn. That word, intimate, hangs in the air.

"Yeah?" My question is nearly a whisper. I clear my throat. Things have gotten sensual so quickly my head spins.

"Yeah. I think I want to hear you say it again. Maybe in another context."

God, he really is sexy. He runs his palm along his sharp jaw, and his burning stare catches me like I'm trapped. *Another context.* Now I know we're both thinking about it. Kissing. Fucking. I'm letting myself fall into the idea, and from the way he's looking at me, he can tell.

"Christine," he whispers.

"Are you ready to go?"

He nods. After we leave—he insists on paying, too—he drives me to my apartment and walks me up to my door.

The wind pushes my hair off my forehead and I pull my coat tighter around me. Eric steps forward. He's waiting for me, I think. For permission.

Several heartbeats pass where I'm deliberating. Should I? I want it—I can't deny that. His lips look so kissable I'm aching with the desire to press my own against them.

Fuck it. I pull on his coat and we fall toward each other. The first touch of our lips shocks me. I feel it all the way to my toes, like an electrical current, and my answering moan emboldens him. He tugs me closer, then kisses me with more fervor. Our tongues tangle.

It's so *good.* I'm melting into the ground as Eric angles his head. We're on fire together. Our hands are wandering a little, stroking through layers of clothing, though his touch might as well be on my naked skin for how carnal it feels.

How long have we been kissing? I'm losing my head as we savor this moment.

I pull back, panting. Eric touches his lips, like he can't believe what just happened.

"That was..." I trail off.

"Yeah." His eyes haven't left me. "I'm going to go home and replay that several times, if it's alright with you."

His honesty shocks me again. He keeps doing that, startling me with how frank he is in his desire for me.

I'm not ready to take this any further, and I can't kiss him again or I'll drag him inside. So instead I lean in to give him a quick peck on the cheek. He must be wearing cologne, and it's divine—oaky, and with a hint of spice I can't place.

"Thanks for dinner," I say.

"You want to do this again soon?"

I nod, even though my heart stutters at the idea. Am I just going to abandon the man I've wanted for several months?

He hugs me before we part.

Back in my apartment, I'm a complete mess.

That was the hottest fucking kiss of my life, and now I don't know how I feel. My clutch lands on the kitchen counter and skids off when I toss it there. I'm flushed, restless, achy. I want to touch myself, but I also want to escape my own head for a while.

Angela isn't home, of course. One never knows where she might be. She could be out doing a distillery tour, or taking a Caribbean dance class, or on a date with someone she met at the indoor music festival she went to last weekend.

A shaky breath leaves me. I want to talk to someone, work this out, so I call my sister. She's the best advice-giver I know.

"Christine? Everything okay?" That's how she answers the phone half the time, like she's prepared to drop everything and run to me if she needs to.

I smile. "Joan. I'm not always in peril when I call you."

Although, truth be told, maybe I am.

I tell her the whole story. She's a little quiet when I'm done, like she's pondering.

"Okay. So the kiss with Eric was hot," she says. "Are you interested in more than just the physical stuff, though?"

"I don't know," I say. "I thought I had the app guy for that. And it's ridiculous, because I don't even know that guy's name."

"You aren't ridiculous," Joan says, so staunchly I giggle. "So try this. When you picture Eric, can you see yourself sitting around with him, doing nothing? That's how I always knew when I was into someone. It didn't matter what we did together, I just wanted to spend time with them. We could sit and stare at a wall for all I cared."

I retrieve my purse from the floor as I pace the living room. "I can definitely see that with Eric. I mean, not staring at a wall. But doing absolutely nothing and enjoying myself."

The picture's hazy, but I envision it: Sunday afternoons on the couch. Doing a crossword puzzle together. Eating pizza on a weeknight when no one feels like cooking.

Why am I still so hesitant?

"So then go on more dates with him," Joan says. "But only if you really want to. You've given him your honesty, and that's all you owe him. And maybe keep in mind that even though app guy said he would meet with you, it's on some nebulous date in the future. You don't have a guarantee that you'll get to explore that."

I walk into my room and sink onto my bed. "You're always a big help, Jo. Thanks."

"Anytime."

I decide not to message my mystery man that night. I'm going to stop tying myself in knots, and maybe the first step is a little distance from someone who clearly isn't interested in me.

I need some time to figure out what I want.

6

———

ERIC

Lucas gives me a ride home after we're done at our Tuesday basketball league. I'm sweaty and tired, but I'm glad for something physical to focus on.

Christine and I have texted a few times, but I'm not sure what she's thinking. I wonder if she's still hung up on the other man. After I asked her, she told me she met him online. That's all I really know. Well, I also know I'm eaten up with jealousy over it, which isn't really fair to anyone, but this burning, awful knot in my stomach isn't hard to identify. Such is being human, I guess.

"So," Lucas says, feigning a casual attitude. "You and Christine, huh?"

I laugh. Lucas is like a nosy neighbor. He's a baseball coach at the high school where I teach biology and chemistry, and we've been friends for a while now. It's impossible not to like the guy.

"I don't know," I say. "I can't tell if it's going anywhere." My cheeks burn.

"You want me to ask Joan about it?"

"No, I do not." I glance at him. "Your meddling is not necessary here."

A good-natured grin stretches across his face. "Fine, fine. I'll just let you figure it out yourself."

He drops me off and I climb the stairs to my place. My phone captures my attention again once I'm inside.

Still nothing from Christine. I messaged her earlier to see if she wants to hang out again this weekend, and she hasn't responded despite our flirty back-and-forth over the last few days. I'm not sure how much more my wretched heart can take, honestly.

I turn the shower on and strip out of my sweaty clothes. The water's already hot by the time I step into it, sluicing in rivulets over my shoulders. I lean a forearm against the wall, mentally replaying, yet again, my kiss with Christine.

Which, my God. It was amazing. In my fantasy, she invites me into her apartment, and I go down on her for as long as she wants before I fuck her slowly. In my imagination, she's—to put it mildly—enthusiastic.

I glance down at my erection and slip my hand around my shaft as I fall deeper into this little vision, wondering how many times I can jerk off to fantasies of her.

I think the answer is: a lot.

In my head, scenes appear one after another. Her hair, a golden brown, hanging down her back. Her smooth skin, peachy now that she's lost her summer tan. Pink lips. A sweet laugh I could play on repeat. The kiss from a few nights ago, something out of my most fervent desires.

I'm stroking a little faster now, breathing hard as I build toward a shuddering climax. Her name, her image, hell, the way her brilliant mind works are at the edge of my thoughts now. My orgasm steals all thought as it hits me.

I lay my head against my forearm. The water's still raining

down on me, so I finish up before drying off and getting dressed.

I really need to move past this. Our kiss was, bar none, one of the hottest moments of my life. She obviously doesn't feel the same way, and I need to learn how to live with that.

A notification greets me when I check my phone again. My stomach sinks when it's not Christine's name, but I *am* glad to hear from Lucy.

It would be better if it was the woman I was just thinking of as I brought myself to orgasm, but still.

> **YourFriendLucy**
> You might have been wondering where I went.

> **ST_Louisville**
> Right to it, I see.

> **ST_Louisville**
> It's okay. I did want to know where you were, but I thought you might need some time.

> **YourFriendLucy**
> Yeah, that's basically it.

> **YourFriendLucy**
> How's it going with your lady?

> **ST_Louisville**
> I thought our time together went spectacularly well, but now I think it might be a bust. Maybe she wasn't feeling it like I was.

> **YourFriendLucy**
> Aw. I'm really sorry.

My thumbs hover over the phone's keyboard. Am I going to do this? I was just thinking about sex with another woman, one I've been half obsessed with for *months*. I finally got to go out with her, and I thought we had a fantastic time.

She's not responding to me, though, and I don't think she's going to. She gave it a chance, and she must have found me wanting. Maybe I should try a little harder to get over her.

> **ST_Louisville**
> I'll be okay. I've had my life on hold for this woman for too long.

> **ST_Louisville**
> So maybe we should meet.

7

———

CHRISTINE

Maybe we should meet.

Those words might as well be engraved in metal for how long they're going to remain imprinted on my mind.

Damn it. I thought I had come to a decision, too: I like Eric, and we had an amazing time together. The kiss we shared ignited every nerve ending in my body.

Now what am I going to do?

> **YourFriendLucy**
> I would still be up for that.

> **YourFriendLucy**
> But first, I'm going to be brave. I'm changing my profile pic to one that's actually of me. That way you know what to expect, and who to look for if we do meet.

I scroll through my photos, searching for a flattering solo shot. One pic in my camera roll features me hugging the enormous bat outside the Louisville slugger museum downtown, which makes me laugh, but doesn't feel right. I land on one from this summer. Joan took it, and in it, I'm wearing a short pink dress and I'm leaning against the wooden fence outside our parents' home. My smile looks happy, and my legs look really long.

YourFriendLucy
Done!

8

———

ERIC

If I had words for how I feel right now, they would include variations of expletives and articulations of a joy and relief so profound I'm not sure I've ever experienced anything like it.

Also, shock. That's what's flooding through me. Because: how in the hell? And what are the chances?

And...did she know? But she couldn't have. We wouldn't have had all this strife if she knew.

Christine's picture stares back at me. I run my thumb over it.

It's unmistakably her. I would know her smile, her long limbs anywhere. Although, now that I think about it, could this be someone who's found Christine's picture? Maybe someone who knows about my interest in her?

That doesn't make sense either, though. She's the one who has pushed for a meeting, and she updated her picture after we agreed to meet. This must be her. Christine. Lucy.

And then I laugh. Because the man she has strong feelings for is *me*. Another shot of elation strikes me.

I think back to our conversations. She has three siblings and a large family. A brother with a disability. She loves sports and math. Her dad and brother were in a car accident earlier this year. Things fall into place.

We have been absolute idiots about this, but we can fix it. Although, in a city the size of Louisville, how could we have known we were taking to each other?

> **ST_Louisville**
> Can you meet tonight?

YourFriendLucy
Wow. We're not wasting any time now, huh?

> **ST_Louisville**
> Is that okay?

YourFriendLucy
Yes. I'm free.

ST_Louisville
There's a coffee shop on Cooper Rd. John's Java House. It's open late since they serve dinner as well. You know it?

It's close to her. My shoulders tense while I wait for her answer.

YourFriendLucy
Yeah, I know where it is.

> **ST_Louisville**
> Meet you there in an hour

YourFriendLucy
Wow. You really are antsy

> **ST_Louisville**
> Yeah, actually. I am.

YourFriendLucy
So who will I be looking for? I want some kind of description here

ST_Louisville
I don't think you'll need it. You'll understand
when I get there.

I pull several shirts out of my closet, not caring when they
land on the bed haphazardly. What article of clothing says,
"hey, I'm the secret man you have feelings for?" I settle on a
white sweater. She might not remember, but she joked once, as
Lucy, that she doesn't like wearing white because she always
ends up with sauce on her shirt.

My heart races in my chest. I hope she still wants me now.

9

———

CHRISTINE

The scent of some kind of savory soup hits me when I walk into the cafe. My stomach rumbles, but I'm too nervous to eat.

It's one of those modern places with the exposed ductwork, Edison bulbs, and high ceilings. The tables are mostly empty save for a few diners.

I stop short when I see who's sitting near the window. "Eric?"

Shit. I can't be on a date with him hanging out at the table next to me. It's completely wrong.

"What are you doing here?" I move closer to him.

His eyes crinkle at the corners. "Wouldn't you like to know."

"I'm meeting someone here," I say quickly.

He smiles again. "I know."

Wait. What the hell does that mean? And he looks *happy* about it.

I stare at him. My mind spins, creating a variety of scenarios, each more implausible than the last. But he's here, and he's grinning at me, and I can't think of anything else that fits.

Holy shit.

I practically fall into the chair in front of him. My purse hits the floor. "Wait. No way." My eyes are wide.

He nods. "Hi, Lucy."

"What the fuck? Did you know?" A wash of dismay covers me.

"No, Christine. I swear. I found out when you changed your picture. Also, do you go by Lucy or something?"

"My middle name is Lucille, and no, I don't really use it. My family calls me Cece if they use a nickname."

He shakes his head. "I guess I didn't know your middle name. If you'd used Cece, I would have put it together, I think. I've heard Lucas call you that. Although, maybe not. It still seems wild, right?"

"Yeah. Wow."

The shock dumping buckets of adrenaline into my system makes me feel like I might have some kind of cardiac event in the middle of this shop. I cover my heart with my hand.

"You okay?" His brow furrows.

"I mean, no. Are you?"

"Yeah, actually." His lips press together.

And now that I'm calming down, I can see this for the wondrous occasion it is. He's my mystery man. And he's Eric, the man I shared an amazing kiss with, the guy I've been ogling for the last few weeks with increasing levels of attraction.

To my dismay, my eyes fill with tears.

"Are you sure you're alright?" He's halfway out of his chair when I look at him.

"Yes," I say, though I cover my lids with my hands. Tears slide down my cheeks. "Eric. How could I have been so stupid?"

"Hey." His hand covers mine. "You aren't stupid. Or if you were, then so am I." His expression becomes contemplative. "Math girl. You're an accountant. I was thinking corporate finance."

"Yeah. I wasn't thinking high school science teacher, either.

And the whole not being born in the US thing went right over my head. Though to be fair, lots of people meet that criteria." I sniffle.

"So," he says, drawing his hand back. He's fidgeting in his seat. "What do you think?"

"About what?"

"You know. Us."

I realize he's nervous because he thinks I might back out now I know it's him. Which is absurd.

"God, Eric. I'm so happy. I've never been this overjoyed in my whole life."

He sags, and I feel awful for keeping him in suspense. I scoot closer to the table.

"I promise, Eric. I wish I had known it was you. We could have saved ourselves a lot of heartache." I study the dusky sky outside the window, then swing my head toward him again. I'm sure my eyes are red, but I don't care. "Were you interested in me at all? As Lucy, I mean?"

"I would have been. Lucy was just overshadowed by Christine for me."

"I felt the same. I like you so much. I just had this unparalleled connection with your online persona. I think we were just more vulnerable with each other there."

"I thought you'd already met the guy you were talking about. On a dating app or something." He laughs. It's a relieved, delighted sound. "You really didn't care what I looked like, huh?"

I shrug. "It felt secondary. I know that sounds nuts, but it's just...I'd never felt like that before. I'm glad you're you, though." My gaze traces over the planes of his face.

We're grinning at each other. The joy bubbles up and cocoons us.

He looks around, as if suddenly remembering something. "You want food, or...?"

"I'm not very hungry," I say. Which isn't true, precisely, but it's not only food I want now.

"Yeah? You want to stay here, then?"

I shake my head.

"Your place is close, right?" His stare turns dark.

"I think my roommate might actually be home for once. Your place?"

"Yes. Yes, my place. You can follow me there."

As soon as we step into his apartment, Eric spins me around and pins me against the door. He stops there for a moment, eyes flitting over my face like he might be mapping my expression and committing it to memory. I'm panting, watching him study me with my heartbeat fluttering and my eyes still stinging from the cold. He's close enough for me to note the scent of his shampoo, something citrusy, and to catch the flecks of gold in his dark brown eyes. His arms are around me, above me, caging me in. He smiles.

Then he kisses me.

We start out tender, soft, just tasting each other. He groans, and the sound is so tortured it's obscene. I find myself moaning, pulling his hips to my own, as I explore his mouth. When we pull back from each other, his tongue darts out to lick his lips. His expression is one of wonder. No one has *ever* looked at me like this, as though he can't believe he gets to touch me.

We come together again, this time with more feverish intensity. My tongue finds his open lips and then we're tangling them together. His hands are wild, first dipping under my coat and then finding the skin at my waist. He's shivering as he crowds me.

"My God, Christine." He has one arm around me now and the other planted near my head.

"I know." I kiss him behind his ear, along his jaw, and he whimpers.

We keep kissing, finding new ways to get closer—his thigh between mine, my arm wound around his back, his hands above my head so he can push his whole body flush with mine.

"Eric," I tell him when he trails kisses over my neck. "I never imagined it could be like this. Not even when we talked about sex. On the app, I mean."

"Jesus Christ," he growls. "If I had known it was *you* talking about how you like to be on top, I would have lost my goddamn mind. Seriously. I can't believe I let that conversation happen without doing something about it."

"You told me something then, too," I say, breathless. "About how you like to go down on women."

He groans again. "I have thought of literally nothing else for months. And no, I'm not exaggerating."

His hard-on digs into my pelvis and his words echo in my mind. I'm a puddle, a weightless cloud, and I've never been so turned on.

"Eric," I moan. I want to root myself to this spot and never leave. He trembles again when I brush his hair off his forehead. "You want me to call you Eric right now?"

"You can call me Seiya," he says quietly. "For this. Feels like that could just be for us."

"Seiya," I say, letting it roll off my tongue.

His answering look is smoldering. He leads me to his bedroom by the hand. My heeled boots clack against his apartment floor. He shucks his coat, then pulls mine off my shoulders, throwing them across a desk chair when we walk into his room. I take a moment to look around.

"So this is where you've been talking to me all this time?"

His bed is made and his room is tidy, other than a few stray shirts, so he's definitely neater than me. The furniture is all a warm brown wood, and his comforter is white. A sleek black desk interrupts one wall. A hint of detergent smell hangs in the air, like he's just washed his sheets.

"Sometimes I was in the living room," he says. "I'm serious though. If I had known it was you...my God, I steered us away from meeting. From talking about sex, or going on dates. I can't believe how much time we wasted."

I put a finger to his lips. "We're here now," I say. He captures my finger with his hand before I can pull away, then tugs me toward him.

We kiss again, another shy exploration that begins gently and escalates the longer we devour each other. His hands are at my waist again, teasing, and I shudder with each pass of his fingertips. From the look in his eyes when he pulls back, he knows what he's doing to me. His molten stare stops all thought in my head.

He starts to tug on my sweater. "Is this okay?"

I nod, reaching for his shirt. "Only if this is okay, too."

"Yes," he says. "Yes, please. Get your hands on me."

He pulls my shirt over my head, and I work his sweater up and over his. I drag my hands over the lean muscle of his smooth chest. He's so sexy I want to drag him down to the bed and never let him go. I'm standing in my pink lace bra, staring at him, and his cheeks are flushed, erection tenting his pants, while he pins his gaze to my body.

"Christine," he whispers.

My arms hang loosely at my sides while he looks me over. His eyes travel the same path over and over, from my neck down to my legs. He lingers over my breasts.

He rakes a hand over his face. "I honestly feel like someone should pinch me. Is this real?"

"I can't believe it either," I say. "I've wanted this for months."

He laughs, then hooks his finger in my waistband to yank me forward. "Yeah? So tell me, who were you picturing on the other end of your phone?"

"Someone hot," I say honestly. "And kind and funny. I was all twisted up over you."

"'Twisted up' doesn't even begin to describe how I've felt about you. I've been a fucking mess."

His touch is tender when he unbuttons my pants and pulls them down. I lay back on his bed while he removes my shoes, then my jeans, and then my socks. For some reason, him taking off my socks is the sweetest, sexiest thing I've ever experienced. He smiles shyly.

He puts his hands behind my knees and tugs me to the edge of the bed. The strength on display, the ease with which he moves me, makes my breath hitch. His arm muscles pop while he positions me, like he's setting himself up for his favorite meal. When he takes off my panties, he sits back, pushing his fist against his mouth.

"Fuck," he mutters. "I'm dying here, Christine."

"I'm going to die if you don't put your mouth on me," I tell him.

He surges up to cover me, kissing his way across my collarbone. He pulls the lace of my bra aside, then lifts me up so he can unhook it, throwing it aside like he can't stand not being against my skin. His lips trail across my breasts and down my stomach. When he puts his mouth to the palm of my hand, kissing the center of it, I quiver.

"God. How can that be so hot?"

He chuckles. His mouth continues the path down, then he's there, licking and teasing my clit like it might be the last thing he ever does. He's ravenous, and it's not long before I'm moaning and writhing.

"Don't hold back," he says. "I've wanted to hear you come apart for so long."

"Oh, God. Eric. Fuck. Seiya." I'm a blubbering mess.

He buries his finger inside me and strokes along the front of my inner wall and then I'm coming apart, crying out his name so loudly that his neighbors are bound to hear.

His hand is still tracing a path over my thighs and hips, a circuit he continues as he looks at me like I might be one of the most amazing creatures he's ever seen. I push my head back into the bed.

"Come here," I say when I sit up again. He hauls himself off his knees to hover over me. "Get these off." I tug at his pants.

He laughs. "Yes, ma'am." After he grabs a condom from his nightstand, he catches my eye again. "You sure you're okay with this?"

"Please," I say, swallowing.

His jeans are on the floor in fewer than five seconds. He moves to his back. He's rolling the condom on as he grits out his next sentence.

"Ride me," he says.

I move to straddle him. "This is the only position that gets me off," I tell him. "I hope you don't get sick of it."

"Christine," he pants. "There is literally no chance of that happening."

I grasp his cock in one hand and sink down onto it.

My exhaled huff of air coincides with his tormented moan. He sinks his fingers into my hips.

"Oh," he says. He clenches his teeth. "Oh, *fuck*. Christ, you feel…"

"I know," I say on another labored breath. "So do you."

We stare at each other. The air stills in the room. I know what we are both thinking: it's too soon to feel like this. We do, though.

I start to move, grinding a little at first, and his hips rock underneath me. I watch as a flush climbs his neck. I use the angle to move my clit on his pubic bone, savoring the little bursts of pleasure wrought from this slow pace. My mouth drops open.

"What else do you need?" he rasps.

I trail my fingers down to touch myself.

"Fuck. That's so fucking hot."

He replaces my fingers with his own, and pretty soon I'm moving faster and he's thrusting underneath me as he moves his fingers. I cry out again when my climax hits. Fireworks light up my brain.

I slump over a little. Eric fidgets from below.

"I really need to come," he whispers.

When I move again, he fucks me harder and faster, lifting up from beneath me and using a tight hand on my shoulder to push me down on him. It's heady, this feeling of power I get from watching him completely lose it, him taking his pleasure from my body with every movement.

His hoarse, low shout when he comes is the sexiest thing I've ever heard.

I slide off him, and he gets rid of the condom. He drapes an arm over me when he comes back to bed.

"I've wanted to be here with you for longer than you know," he says.

"I have too," I say. "I just didn't know it was *you* I wanted."

We're quiet for a minute.

"Now what?" I ask him.

"I don't know. You hungry now?"

I giggle. "No, I mean what are we going to do? About us?"

He rolls toward me. We're still naked, lying on top of his covers. When I shiver, he pulls a throw from the end of his bed over us.

"I want you," he says. "In my bed, in my life, as my girlfriend. I'm not even going to pretend to be chill about it."

I kiss him again and our tongues briefly tangle.

"What about your family? I know you talked about moving closer to them. Is that still in the cards?" My stomach tightens. I would move to another state for this man, a thought that should scare me, but doesn't.

"I want to be wherever you are," he says. "But I'm open to any and all discussions about where that is."

"We're skipping all the early stuff, huh? The dates and all that?"

"Oh, I have dates planned," he says. "I have lots of plans for us, in fact." He mutters something in Japanese.

"Wait. What did you just say?"

"Maybe I'll tell you someday."

"That's not fair." I smile at him. "I'm going to learn the language now, just so you know."

He chuckles.

"Eric."

He watches me, suddenly wary.

"I'm in," I say. "I'm yours. And I'm so glad it was you."

10

ERIC

FOUR MONTHS LATER

I stare at Christine across the bar. Her roommate, Angela, invited us to one of those breakout rooms, which was honestly fun. Then she dragged us out to a bar, which is less fun, but I can't complain too much—I'm watching Christine throw her head back and laugh, her body stunning in a shimmery, floaty dress. I'm flush with the sort of love sickness that mimics a constant, jittery high. My stomach swoops when she's near. Hearing her throaty voice makes it feel like all the blood in my body is moving south.

So, yeah. We've been together for three, almost four months now, and I haven't used the L-word because I don't want to scare her. She's everything, though. She's smart, beautiful, funny—I've never been like this over a woman.

She catches me staring at her, then says something to Angela before coming to talk to me. She doesn't take her eyes off me. Her hair's over her shoulder tonight, leaving her neck exposed, and I want to run my tongue up the line of it.

"Are you ready to go? You look antsy." She takes a prim sip of her drink, a noxious-looking green thing advertised as a St. Patty's day special.

I wrap an arm around her waist and lean toward her ear. "I'm mostly anxious about getting you home," I say, and I'm gratified when she shivers in response. "Also, no offense, but your drink looks kind of disgusting."

She laughs. "It's green apple and it's fucking delicious."

"Are you feeling a little tipsy?"

She pinches her fingers together. "Only a teeny tiny bit. I'm still good to go for, you know."

I raise my eyebrows. "Do I?"

"Come on," she says, leading me away. "I can barely hear you in here." The bar complex is large, and we walk down a hallway and out to the patio, which is hemmed in on all sides by towering walls of brick and ivy. A mural's painted on one side, a graffiti-style, spray-painted scene featuring a racehorse.

It's empty. Though winter's basically over, it's not warm out, and there aren't space heaters out here.

"Now what?" I watch her take another sip of her drink.

"Sit down for a minute." She gestures to one of the chairs.

"Okay. It's kinda cold, though. I don't think we can stay out here for long."

I sit, and she settles onto my lap, facing away from me. There's a table in front of us. I shift around so I can shrug out of my coat and put it over her.

She turns her head toward me and her eyelashes flutter.

"What is it? You're making me nervous."

"I'm being brave," she says. Her chest lifts with her next breath. "I'm in love with you. I just wanted you to know."

My heart shifts.

"It's okay if you aren't ready to say it back," she says.

I turn her face to me. "Christine. You really think I don't feel the same way about you?" I kiss her hard. Our tongues entwine for a moment.

She shrugs.

"I'm so in love with you," I tell her. "It feels like I've been in love with you since we met. It's all I think about. I just didn't want to say it too soon."

When she turns to me, I hope she can see the truth on my face. We kiss again, this time with more heat. We're devouring each other. I start to grow hard underneath her.

She spreads her legs out, panting. "Will you touch me?"

"Fuck, yes," I say.

My fingers trail up her thigh and under her dress to pull her underwear to the side. I drag my finger along her clit and she emits a breathy moan that makes my cock strain in my pants.

She reaches behind her for the button on my jeans, and I put a hand on her arm.

"You sure? Here? Someone could walk out." I'm hanging on to some sanity, though it's leaking out of my brain by the second.

"I'm game if you are," she says, pushing her ass into me, and Jesus do I want this.

I pull my erection out, fumbling a little given our positions, and she lifts her skirt. She positions herself over me, sinking onto me slowly, her wet heat surrounding me. We're bare, and though we've done this before, the feel of it is always a delicious, mind-blowing surprise. I groan next to her ear. She leans forward onto the table.

Just before we can move, someone steps outside. The lady's talking on her cell phone.

We both freeze. My coat still covers us, so the woman shouldn't be able to tell what's happening. Christine sits up, and the sensation of her moving makes me bite back a moan. I grip her hips with shaky hands before she can move again, but even her squeezing and gently shifting has me feeling like I'm going to come.

We wait until the woman goes back inside before we start to grind together.

"I thought she'd never leave," Christine says.

I'm too lost to think about anyone else. "I'm yours," I whisper in her ear on a thrust. "Forever. *I want to be with you forever.*" I mutter that phrase in Japanese.

I find Christine's clit again and I circle it with my thumb until she cries out, squeezing my cock so hard I follow after her in my own orgasm.

She collapses against me. I have no idea what we'll do about the mess we just created, but I don't care.

She captures my lips again. "Forever, huh?"

"Yeah." I chuckle as she pulls off me. "I don't know what came over me."

"I like the sound of it." She tilts her head. "What else did you say?"

"The same thing. And the same thing I said to you the first time we were together. It means 'I want to be with you forever.' I didn't think I should tell you that too early."

We're still looking at each other, and I know we're thinking the same thing. This is it. Forever doesn't even feel like that long.

"I love you, Christine. Lucy. Cece."

"Eric. Seiya. Science boy. I love you, too."

11

CHRISTINE

SIX MONTHS AFTER THAT

Eric
I told you it would be forever.

Eric
By the way, I'm glad you said yes.

> **Christine**
> Of course I did. You're the love of my life,
> mystery man.

> **Christine**
> Also, why are you texting from the living
> room?

Eric
I don't know, it kinda feels like our thing.

Eric
Were you surprised?

> **Christine**
> To find you waiting on one knee after dinner?
> Yes. But after I thought about it, no.

Eric
I adore you.

Christine

ABOUT THE AUTHOR

Did you enjoy this story? You can check out Exactly As You Are, a full length novel in this series, here.

Check out my website! You can sign up for my newsletter and get updates.

www.lilianawoodland.com